House
of
Brittle Bones

Written by:
Jamel Stevens

Cadmus Publishing
www.cadmuspublishing.com

CONTENTS

ACKNOWLEDGMENTS

First and foremost, PEACE to queen Laura Ann, who brought me into existence when she was only 16 years old. May she Rest in Power. I owe a very large debt of gratitude to my grandparents, Edward and Earline Stevens, who raised me since I was a baby. I know I put y'all through hell and inflicted pain. Thank you for your continuous love. Rest in Power, granddad. My beautiful sister, Keva, with whom I've learned some of life's first lessons, thus causing me to develop family social roles of being a big brother.

Salute to my comrades, Anthony Smith, aka Banana, who took me out of the crack game when I was only sixteen and schooled me about the streets. Thank you for never deserting me throughout my troubled life. My 36th street crew; there's too many of y'all to name, so please forgive me.

Sonja G. and Jean Azor. I love the hell out of y'all. Thanks for the support and unconditional love. Hang in there, sis, things get better in time.

Last, but not least, I'd like to acknowledge my haters watching me shine, but always remember; haters make us famous! Peace.

DREAMSCAPE

I hear people screaming my name in my subconscious mind. I feel the rage engage in my conscious mind, saying "Damn, I wonder who I'm going to kill tonight." I stay in my room, thinking of a hundred ways of reaching one's soul by totally mutilating the body. I rip off the muscle complex and subject my hand and wrist through nothing but warm gushing blood, whizzing through the cracks of my fingertips. I feel the heart of my precious prey getting closer as I grab the sack of throbbing muscles in my hand and look up to my sacrifice as she cries and sweats from pain.

In a flash, I awake to find my wife asleep

lying next to me. To my surprise there's a bed of bloodstains and a box of maxi pads on the floor. My nails have the contents of blood.

MAN'S BEST FRIEND

Mr. Jones was an elderly man, whom lived by himself ever since the death of his wife. He lived in a rundown cottage, which was bordered on three sides by a cornfield. The only company that he kept was an old, gray, shabby dog by the name of Rover. He often cried about the death of his wife, and it was as if Rover understood his pain, because he would walk over and lick Mr. Jones' legs, which wore black socks that rose up to his calves.

One day Mr. Jones was sitting in his cottage, rubbing his fingers through Rover's fur.

"Well Rover, I wonder what we gon' eat

tonight. Fish and grits, or some spam?"

He opened his cabinet, which only revealed cobwebs, and not a single can of anything.

Fish was on the menu!

Mr. Jones grabbed his fishing pole and took a deep sigh, and then he and Rover walked out into the world to obtain food.

Later on that evening, Mr. Jones and Rover returned home with two fish inside of a gray pail. Exhausted from travel and work, Mr. Jones plopped down on his rocking chair, which was stationed on the porch. Rover rested at his feet. He started thinking about his wife and how she used to fry up a delicious fish, battered in cornmeal. Within a blink of an eye, dark clouds blocked the sun, turning the glorious afternoon into a sinful hue. Alarmed, Rover raised his head with his ears pointed toward the sky, and took off running into the cornfield.

"Rover! Rover! That crazy dog. What's he up to now?"

After getting out of his rocking chair, Mr. Jones walked into the cornfield in pursuit of Rover. About a minute of walking, Mr. Jones stopped in his tracks by what appeared to be a man standing in his path.

"Hey mister, you seen my dog?"

The man just stood there, staring at Mr. Jones, and did not answer. The man had a straw hat on his head, which covered half of his face, and was parallel to his eyes.

Frustrated and nervous, Mr. Jones tried again, "Mister, did you see a gray dog?"

He walked towards the stranger and was stopped in his tracks once again, but this time from fear and numbness. When he stared down at the stranger's feet, he saw Rover lying motionless.

"He's right here," said the stranger.

Mr. Jones' eyes started to tear up.

"Did you k...kill my dog?"

The stranger did not respond, so Mr. Jones went on: "Please tell me that Rover is okay. I can't live without my dog. Dog is man's best friend."

Shaking his head, the stranger replied, "Must admit, dog is a good friend of man, but not his best friend. Rover gave his life to me in replace of yours. You see, I came for you before, and there was an even greater friend, who recently did the same."

And with that, the Grim Reaper disappeared.

YOU'RE NEVER ALONE

When Tina was thirteen, her mother passed away, leaving Tina's dad to raise her. The two grew a close bond with each other and even planted a Carnation garden (carnations were Tina's favorite flowers). On Tina's twentieth birthday, her father passed away of a heart attack. The house now belonged to Tina, but she could not live in it, for fear that the memories would haunt her. So, she planned to check into a hotel and sell the house to a broker.

A week later, Tina sold the house and was on her way to the airport to catch her flight to Atlanta and start a new life. She decided to stop by the house one last time before leaving. Tears welled in her eyes as she drove up to the house. She could not get out of the car. Tina wanted to at least pluck a Carnation out of the garden that she and her father had planted, but her courage was not with her, so she just drove off.

About an hour later Tina arrived at the airport and took a seat awaiting her flight.

A man walked up to her and asked, "Excuse me, is this seat next to you taken?"

"No, it's not," replied Tina.

Two minutes later a rush of emotions came over Tina and tears started pouring down her face.

"What's wrong?" asked the man passing her a handkerchief.

She wiped her face and said, "Thank you. I just feel so bad because my father died and I sold the house that he raised me in. I sold it to get money to move to Atlanta to start a new life. I just couldn't stay there; the memories would tear me up".

"Well, you have my sympathy. My name

is Garnett" he said, passing her a business card, then added on, "I specialize in spiritual healing".

Tina put the card away and thanked Garnett.

He smiled and replied, "Cheer up, sunshine, flowers don't grow in the dark, perhaps this will cheer you up," he said passing her a brown paper bag, "I have to use the phone."

Tina looked in the bag and saw one of the few things that could possibly cheer her up: A Carnation flower. She looked up to thank Garnett, but he was nowhere in sight.

"Excuse me," she said to a woman, that was sitting behind her. "Did you see where the gentleman went that was just sitting next to me".

"What man? No one has sat next to you since you sat down."

"That can't be," thought Tina, and drew the conclusion that she was probably day dreaming.

Tina remembered that she had taken a card from him and reached for it. Sure enough, it was there. When she looked at the card, she did not see a phone number or an address, just the name that read Garnett O. Demarks. She looked at the initials of his name and started smiling.

THE NIGHT BEFORE

H oliday magic was brewing in my city, seasoned with shoppers that littered the streets. Christmas Eve was finally here. My brother and I were so excited. My family loves the holidays. A day after Thanksgiving, mom and dad always decorate the insides of our house with Christmas ornaments, stockings, and fake snow. My brother and I have the task of decorating the yard, while dad covers the house's exterior with blinking lights.

While we work outside, mom plays Christmas carols from our living room's open window. This year, snow had not yet fallen, so my brother and I only set up the plastic figures of reindeer, elves, and of course, old Saint Nick.

Mom and dad already put a few presents under the Christmas tree, but Santa was supposed to stop by our house tonight to deliver a few more; hopefully my PlayStation. Of course, I already made small tears on the wrapping papers of the presents under the tree. No PlayStation.

Every Christmas Eve we watch Christmas movies and eat a big dinner. Mom always cooked enough food to last for two days (Christmas Eve and Christmas). After a hardy dinner, my brother and I walk upstairs to the bedroom that we share, and prepare for bed. Mom and dad always stay downstairs to clean the dishes and do whatever else it is that parents do.

After changing into our pajamas, we retired to our bunk beds. My brother sleeps on the top bunk and I sleep on the bottom bunk (thanks to my seizures). We excitedly talk about tomorrow morning, when we will run downstairs and tear open our presents. Every year after opening the presents, we dance over to the two stockings that hang by the chimney. My name is on one, my brother's name on the other, would be filled with candy. I don't know at what point in our conversation, but I eventually fell asleep.

I was always a light sleeper and can be awakened by the slightest noise. Whether I was dreaming or imagining things, the sound of glass breaking startled me out of sleep and caused me to sit up in bed. I quietly slipped on my fuzzy bear slippers and looked at my brother who was fast asleep and probably dreaming of candy canes.

I walked to the doorway to listen. I heard someone downstairs.

Mom and dad's bedroom was next to ours, and I could hear snoring coming from inside. Yeah, that's my dad. Maybe mom is downstairs getting a late-night snack. When I walked to my parent's room, I saw both of them lying in the bed. So, if mom and dad are asleep in the bed then that means that the person downstairs is… Santa Claus!

My heart started beating faster and every second was slow motion. I finally reached the stairs and stared down into the descending void. After a few seconds I heard paper rustling and light thudding. I took some deep breaths and gained the courage to ease down the stairs, one step at a time.

Every time a step would creak, I would ease up or position my foot on another spot. Arriving at the bottom, I heard movement and footsteps. Cloaked by darkness, I stood unscathed, hidden in the shadows. I now had the advantage of stealth. All I could really see was the outline of a shape with a giant knapsack on their back… Santa! Its him! I wanted to get a closer look and actually see his face instead of this outline, but fear had me frozen in my tracks. I crept back upstairs and excitedly lay in my bed until I fell asleep.

The next morning, I was awakened by a

shrill emitting from downstairs. It's Christmas morning! I jumped out of bed to wake my brother, and then the both of us ran downstairs barefoot. As soon as we got there, we saw mom and dad in the living room. Mom was crying because the Christmas tree and all of the presents were gone.

YEN AND YANG

A long time ago, Zeus created the heavens and the earth. He then created mankind to dwell on the earth. Mankind loved him and gave him daily praise. This put Zeus in the position of hierarchy, and all of the Gods envied him.

Whenever Zeus would come around, Cupid and Kronos stood in the shadows, speaking hateful of him. What they wouldn't give to have the power that mankind gave Zeus. It would put them in a position of hierarchy.

As the years expanded, so did Kronos' and Cupid's jealousy. One day, the two came up with a plan, which was to give mankind insight and become as one of them. Then, they would stop giving praise to Zeus. Once mankind stopped, then Zeus' rein will diminish.

Kronos decided to approach mankind. Upon the encounter, Kronos gave them a fruit, which he had cast a spell upon. The fruit would increase mankind's' brain power, and he would become Godlike. Upon returning home, Kronos was excited to see Cupid standing at the Enchanted Gates and told him that the mission was successful.

Nine months later, Cupid stormed into Kronos' quarters, yelling obscenities. "You fool, it didn't work! The spell only gave them consciousness and the will power to multiply themselves. Zeus still loves them; and worse of all, they continue to worship Zeus!"

Kronos had a look of disgust on his face. He thought his plan was sure to work.

It was silence amongst the two of them until Kronos looked up at Cupid with a smile on his face and stated, "I have another plan. Pass me your arrows."

Kronos took two arrows from the batch and cast a different spell on the both.

"Now pay close attention, we have to act fast before Zeus starts catching onto our doings. When Zeus is studying mankind, shoot Zeus with this purple arrow." He passed Cupid the purple arrow.

He took a breath and then continued, "Once the arrow hits Zeus, it will fill his heart with hate towards the first person he sees… mankind. Then shoot mankind with this red arrow." He passed Cupid the red arrow and looked around to see if anyone was coming yet. Once mankind is hit, it will cause them to love the first person that they see… mankind. And they will forget about Zeus. Also, the results are permanent.

Cupid waited day in and day out for the right time. And one day that time came. Zeus was studying mankind, and Cupid had to make his move. It was now or never.

He held both arrows in his hands, trying to remember which was which.

Purple or Red.

Red or Purple.

It had to be the red one.

Without another second spared, Cupid shot Zeus with the red arrow. Next, Cupid went to earth and shot mankind with the purple arrow.

Upon returning home, Cupid saw Kronos standing at the Enchanted Gates.

Kronos slapped Cupid across the face. "You idiot, what have you done? You used the wrong arrows. Mankind developed hate amongst themselves and started committing murders, but regardless of their constant fighting, Zeus still love them.

PREDICTIONS

C harles Weatherbee was a weather-
man that worked for a local broad-
casting station. He had been working
for them for the past twenty years. He was
now sixty years old. Lately, all of his weather forecasts had been incorrect. There had
been a lot of complaints from the viewing
population, so his boss Edgar had put him
on probation for the next two weeks.

Once again, his weekly forecasts were
off. His weather temperatures were twenty degrees and he predicted rain when the
days were hot and sunny. Getting close to
firing him, his boss restricted the seven-day
forecast and limited him to a daily forecast.

One day Charles came in and his boss

threatened him with termination if he got one more prediction wrong. That day Charles gave a forecast for a heavy storm.

The next day was sunny and nowhere close to a storm. So, his boss spoke harsh to him.

"You idiot! What are you trying to do, ruin us? You predicted a storm and it's sunny as hell. You're fired! Clear out your stuff!"

Charles went to his locker and grabbed all of his belongings. He pulled a baseball bat from his locker and went into the production room and started smashing cameras and audio equipment. He smashed all of the stage props and furniture.

His boss ran up to him. "What the hell are you doing?"

Charles raised the bat, threatening to hit him. His boss backed up so fast he tripped and fell down. Charles raised the bat at him once again and his boss scattered backwards on the ground into a corner.

Charles started walking towards the door,

but then stopped in his tracks and turned around with a smile on his face. "Here's your f-ing storm."

NIGHT RIDER

Every night dad drives home, drunk as a skunk. Mom always gets on him hard, telling him that one day he was going to kill his fool self. A couple of times my father's drunkenness had caused him to hit other cars, and who knows, maybe even people.

Mom would get on his case until the morning. I bet that was a hangover from hell. Not to mention, my brother and I would jump in the bed with him every time. My mom, so loving and caring, would fix his favorite breakfast every morning.

Scrambled eggs.

Dad loves a lot of onions, so mom would be downstairs chopping onions, and cursing him out as the onions caused her eyes to water tears.

One-night, dad didn't come home. My brother and I ran to his bed and found it empty. When we went downstairs, we saw my mother chopping onions and watering tears. It wasn't until we got close to find out that she was chopping strawberries.

WATCH OVER ME

T he town of Bala had been in an up-
roar due to a series of rapes that
had been taking place. The town
had a population of 200 people. Father
Matthews had called for a town meeting,
which was always held in the church (the
center of town's square). The church was
filled with more noise and chatter than any
Sunday that ever existed.

"Attention! Attention!" shouted Father
Matthews from the podium in the front of
the church.

When the noise died down, Father Matthews continued. "As you all know, the
Devil has been stalking our town and prey-
ing upon the women in our beloved town.

What we must do is implement a curfew and travel in pairs."

Noise erupted from the pews.

"Calm down! Calm down!" yelled Father Matthews.

When the noise died down, 70-year-old Ms. Naomi spoke, "Something else must be done to catch this guy. What if he comes inside my house and tries to make love to me?"

"Shut up, Naomi! What man wants old cobwebs?" stated 60-year-old Ms. Carol.

"Ladies!" yelled Father Matthews with a look of disgust on his face. "We are God-fearing people and the lord has not forgotten about us. In two days, the feds will be in our town to conduct investigations, so until then, travel in pairs. It's always safety in numbers. God sees all, and will protect us. Now let us all depart in peace."

As everyone started to depart and pair up, Father Matthews noticed that Eva was leaving by herself. Eva lived on the outskirts of town.

"Eva, do you need a ride home?"

"Yes, father, I do."

"Well, just wait until everyone clears out, and then I can lock up and drive you home."

About an hour later, they arrived at Eva's house. Her yard was bordered by a white picket wooden fence. The top of the fence was like huge shark teeth. Eva's yard was filled with twenty different statues.

"Wow, you got a little museum going on."

"Yeah, I love art. One of my hobbies is collecting."

"Nice! Well, would you like me to walk you to your front door?"

"No, thank you. I got it from here."

Eva got out of the car and went inside of the house, as Father Matthews watched from behind the steering wheel before pulling off.

Later on that night, Eva was in her bed fast asleep when she was awakened by glass shattering. Not sure if she was dreaming or not, she grabbed a baseball bat that she kept at her bedside, and walked towards the door of her bedroom.

POW!

Something hard socked her in the nose. She dropped the bat and fell to the ground. She was blinded by tears, but still was able to make out what appeared to be a man wearing a mask.

He approached her with a knife in his hands. "Take off your clothes. Now!" his deep voice grumbled.

She felt on the ground for the bat. She finally felt the handle and stood up with a wild swing. Her swing was true; right on the shoulder. The Yankees would have been proud of her.

She swung again. This time spinning the masked man to a full sprint towards the front door. Eva ran back in her bedroom, locked the door, and dialed the police.

The masked man ran out of the front door, sprinting through the statues in the yard. When he got to the picket fence, he tried to hop over, but someone grabbed one of his legs. The masked man was too scared to look back. The more he struggled, the harder he was pulled back. He lost his grip and fell on one of the sharp tips of the picket fence, which went through his stomach. He laid there and died.

When the police arrived at Eva's house, they found the masked man dead, slumped upon the gate. They removed his mask and discovered that it was Father Matthews. One of his shoe laces was caught on a statue of Jesus praying.

THE PRICE IS RIGHT

anice was an east coast city girl that moved to California to pursue her dreams in an economic society. Her whole life was dedicated to her job and climbing the corporate ladder. She neglected family on goings back home; it was all about the money. Janice worked for a united health group called "Atmus". Over the course of 6 years, she had worked her way to a high job position.

Her job was to examine the incoming applications and qualify or deny their medical coverage for surgery. To eradicate biasness, the applicant's paper work did not contain names, addresses, or phone numbers. The info available was the applicant's medical and financials. The name would be replaced by an encoded format of a series of numbers and letters.

Janice was up for a promotion to Vice President, due to her special skills of finding application frauds and also saving her company money in numerous ways. She had to work hard for the next three weeks until her position was solidified.

Every time she denied an applicant, the company would save $20,000 and better. One day, she came into work and studied her lead of applicants. Out of a list of 400, she randomly picked 150 applicants for denial, without even studying the applicant.

Time had passed and the company's President called Janice into his office and congratulated her on a magnificent job on saving money. She was then promoted to Vice President. Janice would now never have to pour over thousands of leads and go through the whole process of investigations.

She decided that she would deny one more applicant for old time sakes. She picked up a sheet of leads and went down the list.

"Eeny"

"Meeny"

"Miny"

"Moe!"

Applicant 5X79! She went to the computer and processed a denial on the application and went home.

About 3 months later, Janice got a phone call from her mother in New York, telling her that her father had just passed away.

A week later, Janice and her mom buried applicant 5X79.

CLOSE ENCOUNTERS

Jessica was a single, middle age, white woman. She lived in a two-bedroom house in Buffalo, New York. It had been snowing all week and Buffalo had received four inches of snow. After a long week of work the weekend had finally arrived. Every weekend she would do her rituals, which was to stay in her pajamas all weekend and watch movies or lay in the bed reading a good book while sipping a glass of wine. Life was grand for a single person.

It was 11 pm on Saturday, and Jessica had been reading and drinking wine all day. She decided to go to the living room to watch a new horror DVD. She gathered covers and created a makeshift bed out of the couch (where she would sleep tonight). The TV was in front of her living room window. She went to put the movie in, but fell in a daze from the beautiful white fluff that coated the landscape.

After a two-minute daze she played the movie, turned the lights off, and got under the covers. The house was dark except for light emitting from the kitchen.

An hour passed by, when Jessica looked up from the television and saw a man holding a knife staring at her through the living room window, looking dead at her. She shrieked loud enough to pierce glass and buried her face under the covers. Reaching in her pajama's top, she grabbed her cell phone and called the police.

Eight minutes later the police arrived at her front door and she told them of someone looking through her living room window. After the police investigated the front yard and the window area, they reported back to Jessica and told her that everything was intact and they did not see any foot prints in the snow. Jessica thought that she may have been imagining things due to all of the wine that she had consumed, not to mention the horror movie.

The police left and Jessica decided to go to her bedroom and get some rest. She turned the television off and went to gather the covers that were left on the couch. Chills went down her spine when she looked in back of the couch and seen a trail of watery footprints.

SAY IT AIN'T SO

There was a black man by the name of Talmud, who was born and raised in Houston, Texas. He was a humanitarian and all about social uplifting. He had just lost his job due to an argument that he had with his boss about politics. Talmud's double-edged sword was so swift, as it cut through the air like that of an experienced lawyer, leaving his boss speechless and unable to rebuttal. His boss fabricated a circumstance, saying that employees were approaching him saying that Talmud was stealing, so the boss had no choice but to fire Talmud.

A week later, Talmud was walking through Galveston beach when he noticed a golden tea kettle sticking out of the sand. He kicked it in mid stride, sending the kettle five feet ahead of him. He went to kick it again, but noticed a rhinestone on it. Talmud bent over to examine it, and to his surprise it wasn't a tea kettle at all. He picked it up, thinking it was some kind of golden treasure. It was kind of dusty, so he started to polish it with his shirt, hoping that he would find a "14k" engraving somewhere. After five rubs…

Poof

There was smoke everywhere and a man with a turban stood before him.

"Greetings, I am the genie of the lamp. Much appreciation is due for setting me free. I am entitled to grant you three wishes."

"Wow, this is unbelievable!"

"Your first wish, sir?"

"Okay, genie, I wish for a mansion right here on this beach."

Poof. Right before his eyes stood a mansion.

"Oh boy, you are real. I didn't really believe you at first."

"Your second wish, sir?"

"Okay, genie, I wish for a billion dollars."

Poof. Right in front of him was five large suitcases filled with money.

"Your third wish, sir?"

Talmud thought hard and long. Then he looked at the genie and said, "I'm tired of all the killing, racism, bigotry, wars, and evil. I wish for World Peace."

Poof.

In the beginning God created the Heavens and Earth, and the Earth was without form and void.

HOUSE AT THE END OF THE BLOCK

here's an old Hag that lives at the end of the block. Rumor has it that she is a witch, and is the cause for all of the missing children in my town for the past forty years. Sometimes the kids in my neighborhood and I throw rocks at her house and run as fast as our little legs will carry us. She lives by herself and has no family members or friends who visit her. Sometimes when we play baseball, the ball accidently lands in her yard, which is the end of the game since no one dared to go in her yard.

One October evening, we decided to throw rocks at her house. Upon arriving in front of her house with a handful of rocks,

Bill dared me to walk on her porch and ring the doorbell. I didn't want to do it, but the girl I had a crush on was standing with us. So, like a fool, I accepted Bill's challenge.

Scared to death, I walked to the fence that bordered her yard. Every second took an eternity. I opened the fence. It creaked so loud that it sent chills down my spine, and drops of pee down my leg. Everything was quiet except for the booming thumps from my heart as I got closer to the door. With every step, the butterflies in my stomach danced to the tempo emitting from my chest cavity.

I'm on the porch and just seconds away from the doorbell. Next to the doorbell is a huge curtained window. Before I can ring the bell, the curtain was snatched open. There I stood, paralyzed and face to face with the witch. I hear my friends scattering and screaming as they left me there for dead. When I turned around and ran for my life, it felt as though everything was in slow motion.

My knees buckled twice, sending me to the ground both times. I stood up on my Jello legs to try to run again, but I twisted my ankle. All I could do was writhe on the ground as the face stared at me through the window.

I tried crawling toward the fence, until I heard the front door open and slam closed. When I turned over to face my fate, I saw the witch coming at me with a Ziplock bag full of transparent magic crystals and a towel. She planned to smother me and suppress my screams.

I made way for the fence, grasping handfuls of grass to propel myself faster. The next thing I know, the witch grabs my left leg. Frantically, I horse-kick my right leg at the same time, letting out an inhumane war cry. I make contact with the center of her face. She drops instantly. From out of nowhere, supernatural strength enters my soul as I stand and run on my sprained ankle until I got home.

The next day, the witch's house was on the news, so I turned the volume up on my television.

In Today's news, the town's oldest resident (Ms. Katy), was found murdered on her front lawn, face busted up badly. The bizarre thing is, in Ms. Katy's possession was a towel and a Ziplock bag full of water.

VENUES

T wo college seniors from different countries had registered with their school's foreign exchange program. They would soon switch places with another senior in a different country for three days. Each would live on the college campus. Bilaal and Grady's name came up in the registry. Neither one had ever left their country.

Bilaal was from a small village in Africa, where the villagers drank brown water from a nearby pond. The village was far from any major city. The villagers had never seen, but only heard of drugs. The college campus was a series of huts. Bilaal sold myrrh and frankincense to the tourist that vacationed at the nearest resort.

Grady was from New York City, where he worked as a waiter at an expensive restaurant. He ate the finest food, and was babied by the spoils of America. He and his friends often got high off cocaine and pills. Drugs were all over the city, and to see people doing drugs in public was a normal thing. Grady's college campus was one of the many buildings that the school had bought.

Two days later both students arrive at their foreign destinations

-Africa-

Grady caught a buggy to the college, where he signed a contract and was given a video to watch of Africa's environment. After watching the video, he traveled to his temporary hut. Upon entering the hut, he felt on the walls for a light switch, but could not find one. He spotted some candles inside of their holders, situated upon a metal plate. Next to the plate was a book of matches, which Grady used to light the candles. He had to go to an outhouse to use the bathroom. He was so scared in the small outhouse, as he listened to the nearby lion's roar and roam freely.

The next morning Grady woke up itching. He had loads of mosquito bites on his body. He was sore all over, due to the haystack that he slept on, which his body was not use to. The haystack was nowhere near the comfort of his bed back home.

Grady did not drink from the pond (which was the village's water source). Just the sight of people drinking the brown water made him sick. He could not find any drugs and everyone that he asked had quickly walked away from him. A student at a nearby hut noticed that Grady was not eating, so he brought Grady a bowl of food and a chunk of bread.

"Eat my brother. You need to keep your strength."

The food smelled great or maybe it was

because Grady had not eaten in a couple of days. Grady ate all of the food. It was so delicious that he sopped the remnant with bread.

"That was so good. What was it?"

"Guano."

"Guano? What's Guano?"

"Bat shit. It's a delicacy here in Africa."

Grady immediately started to vomit.

-New York City-

Bilaal arrived at the college, signed papers, and was escorted to his campus apartment. The lights were left on and Bilaal stared at the light bulb with amazement. It was his first time seeing one. The bed was soft, with pillows made from the finest clouds in heaven. He could not sleep that night, as the light emitting from the light bulb luminated the room. The bed was too soft for his comfort. Bilaal's body was rock hard from years of labor and sleeping on haystacks.

After tossing and turning for an hour, he

decided to step outside for some night air. Bilaal stood in front of his campus apartment, taking in his surroundings, when a man approached him.

"Yo, you got a dollar?"

The man had bloodshot eyes. His face was full of bruises, cuts, and dirt. Straight out of a horror film.

"Here, my brother." Bilaal pulled out a jumble of unorganized bills from his pocket.

The man pulled out a knife and snatched the money. He stood there staring Bilaal in the eyes, daring him to do something. After five seconds of the stare down, the man turned around and ran off. Bilaal stood there in shock, wondering why anyone would do that after he tried to help them.

The three days had passed. Grady and Bilaal were back in their own country.

-New York City-

Grady sat in front of three governing professors of the foreign exchange program. Frustrated, he spoke of his journey.

"Oh my God! It was horrible! There were mosquitoes the size of hornets. The water was nasty and brown, it probably had the E-bola, and on top of that, I literally ate shit. What a nightmare. I'm so happy to be back home where it's safe."

-Africa-

Bilaal sat in front of his professors of the foreign exchange program, with a look of frustration as he spoke of his journey. "It was pure hell! I couldn't even sleep. There were electric candles that never burn out, and a sleeping heap that swallows your entire body when you lie down to try to sleep. In America they are rude. Instead of hunting animals with machetes, they hunt each other with knives. I never want to go back. I am so grateful to be back home where it's safe."

THE MINI VAN

y family and I live in our minivan. We used to live in a beautiful home, but now we are on
the run from a gangster and his goons. The
gangster's name is Mr. Closure. Recently,
mom and dad have been fighting more than
ever and mom wants a divorce. This stress
is killing my eight-year-old brain.

When we were stable, the gangsters used
to call the house, demanding money from
my father. My father would always hang up
on them, then start ranting and cursing. He
owed this gangster a lot of money.

On the morning that we lost our home,
Mr. Closure and his goons showed up and
took all of our belongings, even my toys.

My father gathered us together and escorted us to the minivan. We have been living there since.

Today, my dad was sitting behind the steering wheel, reading a letter. He balled up the letter and threw it on the floor of the minivan's passenger side, where I was sitting. He was pissed. He got out of the minivan to smoke a cigarette, and I grabbed the ball of paper and opened it. It was a letter to the gangster. Written at the bottom of the page was the amount of money that dad and mom argued about owing, and at the top of the page was who it was addressed to…

For closure

DEAR DIARY

Dear Diary,

This the start of my third composition book in two months. I keep the other two in my knapsack. I know that every day I write of killing my Drill Instructor, but I can't help it. Maybe it's the stress of being in these jungles of Cambodia, away from my family, or maybe it's from all of the humiliation and beatings that he gave me. Either way, he's a dead man and will not make it back home.

Look at him, over there sweating like a pig. I should wait until he's fast asleep and kill him in his sleeping bag. As a matter of fact, while his back is currently turned, I should run up on him and choke him to death with his dog tag. What is he doing? Why does he keep looking back at me? He's probably reading porn and doesn't want anybody to know. Anyhow, it's going down tonight. Now he's loading his gun. I bet that I can disarm him and shoot him with his own gun. Hold on a second; let me get a cigarette out of my knapsack.

I'm back! Something odd just happened. I went to get a cigarette from my knapsack, only to find out that it wasn't even my knapsack, it was the Drill Instructor's knapsack. Now this clown is walking towards me with a loaded firearm. Does he think I stole his knapsack? Wait a minute, if I got the Drill Instructor's knapsack, then that means that he has my kn…

SACRED GARDENS

———⟨∘⟩———

*B*REATHE, a voice whispers in my ear. I awake under a tree, surrounded by beauty of pure perfection. What am I? Who are these things that are traveling in pairs, looking just like me? One of them looks rough and burly and the other soft and petit.

I try to make conversation but none of the pairs will speak to me. They only converse with each other. I see a river that parts into four separate rivers, where the things bathe and drink water. Wow, this place is lovely.

A whole day of traveling and I am getting so lonely. Why won't anyone talk to me? All of my worrying summoned a deep sleep to come upon me.

The next morning, I woke up sore, and my side was killing me. I was almost too scared to open my eyes until I felt this soft graze upon my skin which alleviated the pain. I opened my eyes and see one of the soft and petit things that look like me.

"Hi, I am Sophia".

Yes, finally, someone to talk to, now we shall be as one flesh.

The voice spoke again, and Sophia heard it as well.

"I have attached a garden upon your body which you shall carry until eternity. Your gardens have seeds within seeds and shall only be tilled among the two of you."

The voice then went on to explain to me that in the middle of my garden there is a tree that stands upright which will be the foundation for being fruitful and multiplying, and Sophia shall not know any other tree.

One day, I left Sophia alone by one of the

four rivers, and one of the burly and rough things approached Sophia and taught her about landscaping and then tilled her garden, as Sophia consumed the tree within his garden. The next few months, I noticed Sophia growing in size, then something that looked like us crawled out of her garden.

"Come now," said Sophia. "I want to show you a trick. A process called tilling the land and planting seeds."

It was so pleasant and soothing. Now I understood what this garden was that I carried around.

A few months later Sophia grew in size again. Another thing that looked like us crawled out of her garden again.

The voice spoke, "You have disobeyed me, our connection is broken, you shall no longer hear my voice until the days that pass and you will think I am no more."

YOUR PERSONAL JOURNAL

www.ingramcontent.com/pod-product-compliance
Lightning Source LLC
Chambersburg PA
CBHW052143220626
47052CB00005B/1170